GREENE FAMILY VACATION

PIPER RAYNE

Cover Design: By Hang Le

1st Line Editor: Joy Editing

2nd Line Editor: My Brother's Editor

Proofreader: My Brother's Editor

About Greene Family Vacation

Greene Family Vacation Itinerary

Ticket holders:
17 adults. 5 children.

Departs from Anchorage, Alaska
Arrives in Maui, Hawaii

Reports of arguing with the TSA's at the airport, three drunk grandmas, siblings fighting, a tooth fairy, two celebrities, one sunburned redhead, a wild blonde running the halls and one unexpected layover in San Francisco.

Enjoy your trip!

A Greene Family VACATION

Chapter One

Cade

"Sorry, we can't swing it. You'll have to enjoy paradise without us," I tell my siblings at my dad and Marla's house before our Sunday dinner, while we're all sitting around the living room. "We just had Leighton and there's no way we're gonna leave her."

Our family is leaving for Hawaii next month for a much-needed family vacation. When everyone booked the trip, we opted out since Presley was pregnant, but Marla and Hank were supposed to go. After his diagnosis, they offered their tickets to Presley and me. We discussed it but decided to pass. We just had our daughter a couple weeks ago, and we're still settling into parenthood.

"Hank needs to stay put for his treatments." Marla pats my dad's knee.

He gives her the look he's giving everyone these days. Like he's thinking, *Stop talking about me, I'm fine. I do not have prostate cancer.* I guess it's good he's positive though. "I told you I'd delay the treatments."

"NO!" half the room shouts.

Dad shakes his head, continuing to put together a bouncy seat for Leighton.

"But you and Presley go. Leighton will have some quality

grandparent time." Marla reaches into the carrier and tickles her.

"I appreciate that, Marla, but I'm nursing and—"

Nikki cuts off Presley. "I have a pump you can borrow. I'm sure you can get enough to leave for Mom. It's a short trip. Only five days."

Presley and I have already talked about this. We both agreed not to go, but Presley wants me to do most of the talking because she loves my family and hates to be the reason any of them are disappointed. I say screw them, they should understand.

"We're taking the twins," Fisher says.

A few of my siblings pretend that's welcome news, but who really wants to travel with two seven-month-olds? Not me.

"More power to you and Allie, but Leighton is a newborn."

Unfortunately, Marla is probably taking it as an insult that we won't leave Leighton in her care, and my dad is so hell-bent on acting as though he doesn't have cancer he's just as miffed. But they have enough on their plate. After a long nine months of pregnancy, I'd love to spend time with my wife on a Hawaiian beach. What moron wouldn't? But even if Presley wanted to go, I would have been apprehensive. I want to spend time with the baby.

"Plus, this way, I'm here for Truth or Dare," I add.

Jed shoots me a look. One that suggests we've both agreed to let our new manager run the place in our absence. We're supposed to be looking to expand our distribution, open another location while the new manager runs Truth or Dare, but it's only been a few weeks since we brought on Caz. He needs more training, and I need more time to trust him.

"Well, that means we have two extra tickets. Who should we offer them to?" Marla continues being the planner in our family.

Fisher raises his hand. "Cam."

Chevelle groans. "Cam? Why? So we can watch him flirt with half-naked women the whole time?"

"Careful there, you sound jealous." Fisher's voice is low and stern.

Chevelle whips her head around toward him. "You're crazy."

"I better be."

Allie puts her hand on Fisher's knee while bouncing Axel. Something flashes between them that I can't decipher. Do they know something I don't?

"Not to mention Cam can afford his own vacation," Mandi says. "I say we bring Clara."

"I second Clara." Nikki raises her hand.

Presley tentatively raises her hand. "Not sure if I get a vote, but of course, I'd pick my sister. She's had a rough go of it lately."

"Yeah, and mostly due to my moronic brother. We owe her one just for whatever it is he's done." Chevelle eyes Presley. "Even though no one will tell us."

I put my hand around Presley's shoulders. "I'm sure you have secrets we don't know." I point at all the Greene women, and they look down at their laps.

There's been some conflict in the family lately because my stupid-ass brother, Xavier, somehow did something to ruin his friendship of over twenty-five years with Clara Harrison, our town librarian and Presley's sister. Presley knows what went down and she's only shared snippets with me. But what she didn't have to tell me is my brother's rise to stardom from being the starting quarterback for the San Francisco Kingsmen has gone to his head.

We tried to talk some sense into him when he returned earlier this summer to help our dad. I give him props for rising to the occasion, but most of what we said seemed to fall on deaf ears. I think his new and definitely not improved attitude even put his relationship with his model girlfriend at risk. Rumor on the gossip sites is that they broke up, or so my sisters tell me. Now that he's back in San Francisco for training camp, I don't expect to hear much from him and that's just not the Xavier I grew up with.

"Okay, I think we can all agree on Clara." Marla raises her hand, and no one argues. "As for the other ticket, we could offer it to one of Ethel's friends."

"She already has Dori and Midge coming," Posey says. "And who's going to be responsible for those three now that you and Hank aren't going?"

Marla looks at my dad. "Well, one of you will have to."

Mandi quickly raises her hand. "Not me. I know I'm the easy choice since I'm usually the responsible one out of us, but I am not going to spend my week away from the inn babysitting three elderly women who will badger me about being single, embarrass me by trying to fix me up, or having to talk the police out of arresting Midge for theft."

No one says anything because we all assumed it would be Mandi, and let's face it, it'll probably still be her because no one else will step up.

"Maybe we can make up a schedule. Each of us takes a day or something," Allie offers, and Fisher snorts.

"We have our hands full," he says, staring at Axel on her lap. Laurie is currently propped up with two pillows because she's already sitting up and poor Axel isn't. I can already see that the comparisons those two will have to endure their whole lives will be insane. "There is no one else. Cam is practically family."

"But he's not," Chevelle says, and the way she keeps fighting this has my senses tingling that maybe there's more going on I don't know about. "Rylan can bring another friend. I'll even watch them."

"One is enough, and the only friend who was even allowed to go is Declan." Marla shakes her head. "Maybe Cam wouldn't be a bad choice. He could help watch the boys."

Everyone laughs. Cam in charge of the boys? What planet did she just arrive from?

"Calista," Nikki says and eyes Rylan across the room.

He only gives her a disgusted look.

"No girls," Marla says and pats Rylan's knee as though he wanted Calista to come. "I think Hank and I will just make the decision." She looks at my dad, who is busy on his phone. Probably playing Words With Friends, as he seems to do that a lot these days. "Hank?"

"Cam," he answers without looking up from his phone. "He's like family."

"He *is* family," Fisher says and eyes Chevelle.

She throws herself back in her chair and blows out a breath. She's always hated losing, but I can't decide if there's more to it than that.

This feels like a family vacation that'll go down in the books. I'm kind of relieved I'll be missing it.

Mandi

e're at the airport, standing in line to check in, when my phone dings with a text message.

Grandma Ethel: Be a dear and meet us at Departure.

I groan and look at my siblings—none of whom have reached for their phone. Of course she would only message me.

"Grandma Ethel needs help unloading all their stuff. I think one of the guys should go."

No one even glances my way.

Who am I kidding?

Adam and Lucy have their foster child, Trey, who they had to get special permission to bring. He's never flown before and is freaking out.

Jed and Molly have Emelia, who's upset about a stuffed animal she forgot.

Fisher and Allie have the twins. Enough said.

And Gavin is on the phone, talking to a Sunrise Bay resident about a complaint regarding something going down at City Hall.

"I'll go with you," Clara says from beside me.

We tell my siblings to watch our bags. Chevelle gives a nod as she's posting on social media, and Nikki assures us we're good.

"I knew I'd be stuck on grandma duty," I grumble.

"They aren't that bad. They can be kind of sweet. Ethel asked me to take some books over to the retirement community, so I picked a variety I thought would interest them."

"And?" I raise my eyebrows as we exit the airport onto the crowded sidewalk at departures.

"She put an anonymous complaint box out and three people complained that they wanted dirtier stuff. One specifically asked for the book with the red room."

I shake my head. "Is that going to happen to us when we get old?"

"That we become hornier than we were as teenagers?" Clara asks. "If we go off of that retirement home, then yes."

We both laugh and look around, but as soon as we hear their voices, our laughter abruptly stops.

"I told you, I got it." Midge is tearing a bag away from one of the skycaps.

"Midge, he's just trying to help," my grandma says.

"This has all my medicine in it."

The skycap puts up both hands and another guy steps in. He has his back to me, but looks familiar nonetheless.

"Who is that?" Clara whispers while we approach the Bronco the ladies are gathered around.

"I don't know, but that ass."

Clara makes a noise of agreement.

The guy is all muscle. Well over six foot three, broad shoulders that stretch the fabric of his T-shirt. He has longer dark hair that's pulled back from his face and he's wearing pants, though I have no idea how in August. Sure, it's Alaska, but if you're a true Alaskanite, then no way can you stand jeans in the hottest month of summer. This is what we wait for all year. So it stands out to me that he'd be wearing pants. Maybe he cranks the air conditioning in the car all day for his passengers?

"Relax, Noah, I'm fine." Midge pushes past him, dodging his shoulder and causing him to spin around.

"Oh," I say and stop.

My eyes lock with his for a moment.

Clara stops walking and looks between us. "Do you know him?"

"It's Noah. He's a photographer. Sometimes he stays at the inn."

"Mandi." Noah's smile is immediate, and it warms something inside me as it always does. A spot that's been cold for a very long time. "What are you doing here?"

I signal to the grandmas who are still arguing with the skycap. "I'm getting them."

Clara rushes over to help clear up whatever the problem is, informing the skycap what flight they're on. She pretty much handles it like a pro, and I barely have to intervene except to tell Ethel she can't take her knitting needles in her carry-on.

"I'm not going to stab someone," she says.

Noah clears his throat behind me, and I turn to face him. My neck cranes from looking up. One thing I love about Noah is he makes me feel small.

"Is this some volunteer thing?" he asks.

I laugh. "Like I'd voluntarily agree to take three elderly women to Hawaii to be badgered about being—" I'm quick to cut off what I was saying. He probably knows I'm single.

"Noah, thanks for the ride." Dori pats his cheek. "Next time though, fifteen minutes before planned. You never know with traffic."

Noah halfheartedly smiles at her. "Got it, Bluehaze."

Dori laughs and shakes her head. "The nicknames and this guy." She thumbs in his direction.

"Hi, I'm Clara." She extends her hand, but Noah's eyes only briefly meet hers as they shake hands.

"You're a volunteer too?" he asks, then his attention is back on me.

"Noah thinks we're chaperoning Ethel and her friends willingly," I say with a smile.

Clara giggles. "Sure, I've got a suitcase full of Bengay and overnight diapers."

"If not just being nice, what gives?" His forehead wrinkles a little.

"It's a Greene family vacation and my grandma"—I point in her direction—"invited her two friends to come along. She said she can't keep up with all our energy, so she needs friends to play cards with."

"Which really means to gossip and get into trouble with," Clara adds.

"You two both single?" He points his finger between us.

I groan. "Unfortunately, yes."

He touches my arm. "I'm sorry. Every available man will know within five minutes of you arriving at the hotel."

"Right?" I cringe. "I could stow you away. We could always pretend."

We all laugh.

"This was one ride you should have declined, right?" Clara says.

"What do you mean?" Noah asks Clara.

"You're their Uber driver, no?"

"No." He shakes his head. "I'm Midge's grandson."

"Oh," Clara says.

As if Midge heard us, she comes over. "Bend down so I can kiss your cheek."

Noah does as his grandma asks, and she leaves her signature berry-pink lipstick on his cheek.

"Be a good boy while I'm gone. No excursions?"

Noah looks at me out the corner of his eye then back down at her. "Not until October."

"Good. I like you being home."

"Where's home?" I always thought he lived on the road, hence the reason he stays at the inn sometimes for lengthy visits.

"Greywall of course," Midge says in a tone that implies I'm stupid.

Clara and I look at one another and raise our eyebrows.

"We gotta go," Ethel says from the entrance of the airport, forcing everyone else trying to enter to walk around her. "Thanks, Noah. See you on the flip side."

"Flip side?" I mouth.

Noah laughs. "Have fun, you two. Too bad there's not an extra ticket."

"Yeah, too bad," I say more in a whisper.

"Nice meeting you, Noah. Wish us luck," Clara says.

We both raise our hands in a goodbye and turn around.

"Holy shit, that guy likes you," Clara whispers, staring over her shoulder one more time as though we're thirteen.

"He does not. He just—"

"Why would he stay at the inn if Greywall is home if he didn't like you?" Clara asks about the same thing that piqued my interest the minute I heard it.

When we reach the sliding doors, I turn around one last time. Noah is watching us, and he puts up his hand in a quick wave with a smile that lights up my insides. It's a magical moment—until the traffic officer yells at him to move his truck.

"Oh my God, you like him too! You like a guy with the same name as your nephew. This should be fun."

I just roll my eyes at her.

Once inside, we return to the check-in with the family, they're all at the front desk, and our suitcases are being tagged and taken away by airport security.

"Whoa!" I yell, and Clara and I rush over to stop them. "These are ours."

The security officer takes us aside and makes us show identification, asking us why the bags were left unattended, and I explain that they were left under the care of our family members.

"Do you not listen to the announcements over the loudspeaker? Do not leave your bag unattended." The woman pronounces every word as if we're idiots for entrusting our family with two bags. Which given our current circumstance, maybe we are.

"We're very sorry," Clara says.

She drops both bags on their sides. "You need to go through them now. Make sure nothing's been added before you check in."

Clara and I squat, unzipping our suitcases while the security officer stares over our shoulders. *I'm going to kill Chevelle and Nikki for this.*

After we've checked there's nothing we didn't pack inside, we're allowed to go.

"Thank goodness we got to keep our bags," Clara says while we wait in line.

"I know. I would've had to spend the trip in men's clothes probably. You know how hard it is to find cute plus-sized clothes? Especially a bathing suit?" I shake my head and almost cry just thinking about how much that would've ruined my vacation.

Clara doesn't say much because she could easily go to the gift shop or anywhere else and find cute clothes that fit her. Not that I resent that fact, but finding plus-sized clothes in a resort area wouldn't have been easy.

Finally, we check in and laugh at a pissed-off Fisher, who's being held up at security, and hightail it to the gate so I can give Chevelle and Nikki a piece of my mind.

Fisher

"With all due respect, I'm a sheriff. I can assure you there's nothing under my baby in her car seat." I run my hand through my hair.

"I can take her out. I'm sure she'll stay asleep." Allie moves toward the car seat, but I put my arm out to stop her.

This is between this TSA supervisor and me now.

"It's protocol. All these things have to be wanded," he says, staring at me through his wire glasses.

I pull out my badge. "We're on the same team."

He glances down but clearly isn't impressed. "Rules are rules, as I'm sure you're aware."

"Listen." I lower my voice and lean forward. "I've been up half the night with this one. She's teething and she's finally asleep. I want to get her on that plane and have her stay asleep if at all possible so I can sleep. You get me? Are you a father?"

He nods. "I am."

"Then I'm sure you understand."

"I do."

"Then we can keep her in the seat."

"No." He crosses his arms.

I growl, and Allie steps in front of me. "The last thing we

need is for you to get arrested." She smiles nicely at the TSA guy and unbuckles Laurie, carefully taking her out. "Here."

There's the edge to her tone. The one I fucking love. The one that says she's on my side, but we have to play by the rules.

The TSA guy wands the car seat and Allie walks through the metal detector with Laurie in her arms. The agent puts the car seat through. I hold Axel, who is all smiles and probably making everyone think his dad isn't a complete asshole. The group behind us claps and I flip them off on my way through the metal detector.

Once we have the two kids back in their car seats and in the stroller, I wonder why we're doing this. Maybe Cade and Presley had the right idea. I wheel them toward the gate as Allie asks if I mind if she pops into one of the stores to grab a magazine on the off chance the babies sleep.

"Take your time," I tell her.

"You sure? I don't want to have to go down to some security office to spring you instead of being on a beach in Hawaii."

I chuckle and look at both our kids, who are wide awake. "It's all good. I promise to behave myself until tonight... in the bedroom."

She stares at me for a beat and lets a few people pass by so no one hears her reply. "Did you enlist your siblings to babysit or something? Last I checked, we're in a room with two Pack 'n Plays."

"I promise, I'll make it happen."

She nods, clearly disbelieving me, and saunters into the shop. I watch her with a voraciously as if she's not my fiancée. Man, I got lucky.

I head to the gate but get stopped by, no shit, five different people oohing and aahing over my little ones. I mean, yeah, they're gorgeous, but let a man get to where he needs to be. By the time I'm sitting with my siblings, I flip off Mandi and Clara for leaving me high and dry at security.

"We were waiting for an announcement to come on overhead that said the family of Fisher Greene had to meet him outside the airport." Jed laughs and leans back in the uncomfortable airport seat.

I rock the stroller back and forth in front of me. "One day when your kid doesn't show up as a five-year-old, you'll understand the phrase don't wake a sleeping baby."

"Low blow," Jed says with a scowl, and Molly nods in agreement.

I look at their daughter, Emelia, who is now seven and sitting with Adam and Lucy's foster kid, Trey. They're playing some dice game all by themselves in the corner while I have Laurie giving me that face that says she's about a minute away from screaming if I don't take her out of the seat.

When we found out we were having a girl and boy, I assumed the girl would be like Allie and the boy like me. But nope. Axel is all smiles, laughter, and happiness, just like his mom. While Laurie is crabby, impatient, and a little cranky, just like me.

Getting ahead of the game, I unstrap Laurie from her car seat and bring her to my lap. Axel chills and swats the things dangling down off his car seat. Everything is calm until a cart arrives and drops off the grandma crew.

"Grandma, I've been calling you," Mandi says. "I led you through security well before anyone else."

"Didn't you see that cute tavern? Midge is Irish, so we stopped." My grandma shrugs.

We all share a look. No way we're about to board a plane with three drunk grandmas.

"Did you drink?" Mandi asks, sounding a little incredulous. She's always taken on a motherly role more than any of us.

"No." But all three giggle as if they're eighteen years old.

"What the fuck?" Jed mouths to me. "Bibi, if you're drunk, they won't let you on the plane."

"What does drunk mean?" Emelia asks from where she's playing.

"Nothing." Jed shushes her.

Emelia goes back to playing her game, telling Trey that her dad says a lot of bad words, so she thinks drunk is something she's not supposed to repeat.

"One beer is not drunk. In case you've forgotten, we're all older than you." Ethel points around at the entire crew gathered by the gate.

They sit down and start pecking at Mandi about Midge's grandson, Noah. She's quickly annoyed, and I don't blame her.

"When are we boarding?" I turn to check and see the attendant opening the doors behind the standing desk. No way I'm missing the early boarding call for people with young children.

I stand and look down the corridor. The crowd isn't too thick, but there's no sign of Allie.

"Come on, Emelia, pack up," Molly says, obviously having the same plan I do. "Maybe we can tell them how upset you are about leaving your stuffed puffin at home and they'll let us on early."

"You too, Trey." Lucy is quick to follow suit.

"Just so you two know, we're going first. We've got more to handle," I say to both of them.

"Right, so doesn't it make more sense for us to go first?

We can be seated while you're still arguing about checking the stroller," Adam says, laughing with Lucy.

"As if you guys don't have it easy. You don't have to board with those two. Give me a break."

Adam leans in. "Trey is worried, okay? This is his first plane ride."

"What a coincidence, it's the twins' first time on a plane too," I say.

"Except they don't know it," Adam says.

I narrow my eyes. "Are you calling my kids stupid?"

"I'm calling them seven months old!" Adam shouts, then lowers his voice. "We've all got issues, they're just not the same. Doesn't mean one is harder than the other."

I hate when my little brother schools me and makes sense. Although I'll never admit it to him.

"Where is Allie anyway?" Adam asks.

The attendant comes over the speaker and announces early boarding. All three grandmas stand.

"What the hell?" I ask.

Grandma turns around. "It's for the elderly *and* the young, Fisher. Watch your mouth before I wash it out with soap. Your father and Marla aren't here to discipline you, so I'll do it."

My forehead scrunches. "I don't get disciplined. What with me being thirty-two now."

She leans in close, and I smell the beer on her breath. "You're never too old for me to take you over my knee."

It's a threat she's used my whole life and never executed once. But she's my grandma and I have to respect her, so I nod and mumble, "Sorry."

I pull out my phone and dial Allie. No answer. Well, regardless, I'm getting situated on this plane before I have to deal with the crush of passengers, so I walk over to the boarding attendant. "My fiancée is at the shop down the way. I gotta get these two boarded, but I have her ticket. Any way I can leave it here with you?"

She raises her eyebrows. "No, sir. I assure you, you'll get boarded just fine without the extra time."

While I stand there stewing, the three grandmas walk past me, actually poking Laurie in the stomach and speaking baby talk.

"See you on the plane." Jed winks, and his family heads through the door into the tunnel.

"Are you sure she's coming?" Adam raises both eyebrows, wearing a smirk that any other time I'd wrestle off him. But I'm probably already being followed on camera as the bragging sheriff who might be a problem.

Logan slaps me on the back when he and Nikki follow my other two siblings and their families to the plane. "See you on there."

Adam's words ring in my ear. I don't usually doubt my fiancée, but things at our house have been rough with Laurie teething. We've been arguing more than usual. I've been a bigger prick than usual. Damn it. I should've brought her flowers or something.

They open the boarding for certain zones and everyone else in our party stands. I feel like an angry bear, but I pretend it doesn't bother me as I rock Laurie and try to keep Axel entertained.

No way Allie left me. I'm just being paranoid. But as I watch more and more passengers board the plane and she doesn't answer her cell phone—again—my insecurity gets the best of me.

I'd probably leave me too, but she'd never leave the kids. Damn, am I going to be one of those stories that breaks people's hearts? *She just left him at the airport when they were supposed to be going to Hawaii as a family.* My mind spirals, picturing me as a single father of two, five or ten years down the line. Would people assume the worst? That I was a cheater or some asshole who hit her? Or the classic, a one-night stand who broke up. They tried to make it work for the kids.

"Oh my god!" Allie says next to me, catching her breath and yanking me out of my worst fucking nightmare and back to reality. She reaches for Laurie. "I'm so sorry."

I hand off Laurie and we situate her in the car seat, then we take Axel's car seat out and fold up the stroller to be checked. I don't say much to Allie until we're seated. Both of us are on the aisle with a car seat next to us. I'm sure the strangers by the windows hate us.

"I'm so sorry," she says across the aisle. "They didn't have the gum you like, and the woman told me they sell it at some other store farther down." She reaches into her bag then hands me a package of gum. Sure enough, it's my favorite gum. I stare at her for a long moment, causing her to continue rambling. "With the airplane and the pressure, I thought you'd want it. I remember you telling me once that flying really bothered your ears."

I lean across the aisle, putting my hand behind her neck and pulling her toward me. "I fucking love you," I murmur before I kiss her so thoroughly her knees should be quaking. "I'm sorry I'm a prick sometimes, but I love you."

She chuckles and draws back, her hand on my cheek. "What did I miss?"

I shake my head. "Nothing. I just want to make sure you know that in my life, the sun rises and sets on you."

"I know." She laughs again. "Remind me to buy you gum more often."

I kiss her one more time before the flight attendant

clears her throat and interrupts us. We strap in, and I pop a piece of gum in my mouth right before the pilot announces that we've been cleared for takeoff. I lay my head back, knowing how lucky I am to have Allie as the mother of my children and my soon-to-be wife. Best fucking surprise of my life.

Then Laurie wails. Somehow, I'm calmer than I thought I'd be. All thanks to Allie.

Chapter Four

Chevelle

The minute we step onto the resort, I realize this is the life I was meant to live. When I spot all the tanned, shirtless men walking around, it only cements my belief.

"Hey," an attractive guy says, clearly looking me up and down as he strolls by.

"Hi." I give a little wave.

"Seriously, you're going to go for a meathead?" Cam asks, distracting me from watching the stranger go by.

I shove him and he pretends I'm strong enough to actually move him. "He's not a meathead."

"Sorry... surfer."

"What's wrong with a surfer?" I raise an eyebrow at him.

"Chances are he can't even hold down a job and lives at the beach, probably smoking weed."

"You're stereotyping. They'd probably take one look at you and think you're some hunter/fisherman who kills every animal he comes across and lives in an igloo."

He shakes his head. "I'm just saying, you'd eat up a guy like that."

We both look over to where the guy has now joined his friends. They're all in board shorts and shoeless, talking to the concierge as though they know him well.

"What's that supposed to mean?"

Cam opens his mouth to answer, but I overhear the rest of my family figuring out the rooms.

"Chevelle can stay with Grandma Ethel then," Nikki says.

I whip around, forgetting whatever Cam was saying. "I'm sorry?"

"We're just figuring out the rooms. We couldn't book another room, so this way everyone has their own bed." Nikki fills me in on a plan that I am not down with.

Grandma puts her arm around my waist and pulls me toward her. "This will be so much fun. Just us girls. Like a prolonged sleepover. Remember when you used to love to sleep over at the house?"

I fake a smile. "Yeah." Meanwhile, I give a death stare to all my other family members until I remember... I turn and eye Cam. "Who are you staying with?"

He chuckles and glances at Fisher. "Myself."

Cam goes around our group to the other receptionist and hands over his credit card and ID.

"What? He got a room to himself?" I'm this close to stomping my foot like a three-year-old.

My sister nods. "He got his own room."

"And why didn't I?"

"No one thought about it until we got here, and there are no other rooms available." Nikki puts her hand on my arm like Marla does when she feels as though she's disappointed us. "I'm sorry. I'm usually on top of these things, but with the baby... I'm not myself these days."

Since she looks as if she's seconds from crying, I suck it up. "It's okay. Yay! A sleepover." I look at my grandma and drum up the best smile I can.

We all get our keys and head to our rooms. They're scattered around the resort except for mine and my grandma's and Dori and Midge's. Lucky for me, they booked adjoining rooms.

"Now, Chevelle, honey, I hope I don't wake you. I can be an early riser," Grandma says while we look for the room.

"That's okay. I want to experience as much as I can while we're here. I'm game for being up early."

"We should go for a walk on the beach," Dori says.

"Pick up seashells," Midge adds.

"It'll be so fun. Just four gals hanging out in Hawaii." My grandma pats my shoulder.

I cringe more than smile, I think. What I really want to do is learn how to surf and hang out at the pool bar and meet some hotties.

"So fun. I'm going to go change." I use the key card to get into our room.

The minute we get inside, Grandma opens the adjoining door, knocking on the other. Midge opens the door on their side and acts surprised, pushing up her dark-rimmed glasses. They both pretend to be scared and I have to admit it's kind of cute the way they are with each other.

I drop my suitcase on one of the beds and pull my bikini out of the front zippered pocket. I wanted to be prepared in case we couldn't get into our rooms right away. Heading into the bathroom, I lock the door. I shaved all my bits and pieces last night, so I'm ready to go. I'm making the most out of these five days. I walk out of the bathroom and throw the clothes I was wearing on my suitcase.

Grandma is busy hanging up her clothes in the closet. "Chevelle!"

Grandma has never said a word about my clothes. She's usually the one telling me to flaunt it as long as I have it. But it's clear from her tone that she doesn't approve of my bikini.

"I can see..." She points at my general chest area.

"It's called side boob."

"But..."

"Believe me, Grandma, it's very trendy right now."

She nods, still staring in disbelief. "I can't imagine if your grandpa ever saw it. He'd probably lock you up in the attic."

I laugh and pull out my sunblock, hat, and book I won't have time to read... if I'm lucky. "See you ladies later." I open the door.

"You're not going to wait for us?" Midge peeks her head into our room. "Oh, wow." Her gaze goes to Grandma, who just shrugs.

"I'll see you down there." I wave and let the door close behind me.

When I reach the elevator, I press the button to go down. Luck must be on my side, because I don't have to wait long before the elevator arrives. Except when the doors open, Cam is standing there wearing his swimsuit and sandals. Only his swimsuit and sandals.

Cam has been Fisher's best friend forever, so of course, I've seen his naked chest, but probably not since last summer. The past year has been good to him. He's as chiseled and muscular as ever with a trickle of dark hair from his navel that leads to under his shorts.

"Great minds think alike," he says, holding the door open button. "You gonna join me, or are you just gonna stare at me all day?"

Somehow, I manage to strip my eyes off his physical perfection and narrow my eyes. "I'm not staring at anything except your fake tan." I step into the elevator with the usual chip on my shoulder Cam seems to put there.

He scoffs. "Fake? Try working on the dock every day this summer."

"You? Work outside? I must've missed it. I thought the bosses just sat up in their air-conditioned offices and watched the rest of us work?"

He faces me and leans back against the elevator wall. "I invite you to shadow me someday then."

"Gladly." I cross my arms.

"Just so you know, your arms don't hide anything." He stares at my cleavage.

"I'm not trying to hide anything."

"Clearly."

I place my arms at my sides. The hungry need in his eyes unnerves me because I like it.

The elevator door opens a few moments later and he steps out in front of me, which is not something he usually does. Sure, Cam can be a little brash and rough around the edges, but his mom raised him right. He's usually a gentleman.

I follow him to the pool, admiring his body, shaming myself, then admiring him again. His ass is perfect, and the way his back muscles bunch and flex as he swings his arms makes me bite my lower lip. I can't even think about the *V* shape on his abdomen without my mouth watering.

Lord, I must really need to get laid if I'm fantasizing about Cam.

We both end up at the pool and there are no other Greenes in sight. I grab a towel and walk past Cam, setting myself up on a lounger by the bar. I lay out my towel, apply sunblock, and put on my hat, starting the book I grabbed from Hank and Marla's. She's been on a reading kick since Hank's been sick.

Cam sets up at the bar as I figured he would, making

friends immediately as he always does. Let's be honest, the only reason he and Fisher are friends is because Cam is Cam. A guy's guy who everyone loves—most women included.

Every time I turn the page, I glance up and our eyes connect, but I continue reading my book, sweating my ass off because damn, this heat is intense. I thought Alaska was hot right now, but it's nothing compared to this tropical paradise in the middle of the ocean.

When I'm about ten pages into a book that I have no idea what it's about, a dark shadow appears over me and I figure, *bingo*, I've hooked a guy's interest. I lower my sunglasses and look up over the rim, only to find Cam holding two fruity-looking drinks with umbrellas in them.

"What are you doing?" I seethe.

"Thought you might be thirsty?"

He sits on the lounger at my side and sets both drinks on the table between us.

I glance at the bar and almost everyone is looking, but they quickly turn away. "What did you do?"

"Well, since you decided to make a spectacle of yourself, the guys at the bar were all betting who could get a date with you."

I stare blankly, so he continues.

"And of course, I told them you aren't available."

"Cam!" I whisper-shout. "What did you tell them?"

He shrugs his muscled shoulder. "I told them you're my girlfriend, but we're keeping things on the down low because we're here with your family. And I'm your brother's best friend and..."

I hold my hand up to get him to stop. "Why would you do that?"

He looks at me as though it should be obvious. "They're only looking for one thing."

"I'm only looking for one thing!"

He rolls his eyes. "Trust me, you dodged a bullet. They were talking about your ass, your breasts. They're only interested in your body." He sips his drink and raises it toward them.

They all laugh and quickly turn as soon as I look.

"So what?"

"Come on, Chevelle, there's more to you than just that, as much as you try to hide it. You need someone who loves your mind too. Your brothers would kill me if I let you sleep with one of those douchebags."

"*I'm* going to kill you," I whisper. I swing my legs over to get up, but I'm stopped by someone shouting my name.

"CHEVELLE!" Grandma is on the other side of the pool, waving.

She and her friends are wearing swimsuits with skirts and hair caps. They have their own towels instead of the hotel towels, and they're walking toward me.

"I better go. The family isn't supposed to know we're dating." Cam winks and hurries back to the bar, complimenting Grandma and her friends on their suits.

"Glad we saw you. It's kind of crowded." Grandma smiles and looks at the three loungers.

"Oh, you saved us seats. What a gal pal you are," Midge says.

"That's me, just one of the gals." And apparently Cam's pretend secret girlfriend.

I'm half tempted to tell him there are certain obligations that come along with a fake relationship that he's going to be responsible for if he keeps all the available men away.

Adam

We've been here only a day and I'm not sure I ever want to leave. Sitting poolside with my wife while watching Trey play with Emelia is about as good as it gets. Those two have found a friendship I didn't expect but appreciate.

"I lost my tooth!" Trey runs over to us, holding his tooth, a big bloody smile on display.

"Whoa," I say, sitting him next to me on the lounger.

He hands Lucy his tooth, and she beams with excitement.

When Trey came to us, it was clear he didn't believe in Santa Claus or the Easter Bunny, so I'm sure the Tooth Fairy is on the list. But I see the hopefulness in Lucy's eyes. The one that says this is our chance to prove it to him. But he's already lost teeth before he came to us and I'm pretty sure the Tooth Fairy didn't come then unless he happened to be staying at another foster family's house and even then, who knows?

While I use a napkin left over from our poolside snacks to get the blood to stop, Lucy says, "We'll have to put it under your pillow so the Tooth Fairy will come."

Trey says nothing. If anything's been clear over these last several months, it's that he doesn't want to disappoint Lucy.

Lucy bends down. "I know the Tooth Fairy has had a hard time finding you in the past, but I guarantee she'll find you this time."

Trey looks up. "In Hawaii? We don't even live here."

"The Tooth Fairy travels," I say, shaking his shoulders a little, hoping to transfer some of my own excitement to him.

"Doubtful." He takes the tooth from Lucy, inspects it for a second, and tosses it in the bushes behind us.

"Trey!" Lucy yelps, rushing over to the bushes.

"Did you show them?" Emelia comes over, dripping wet from the pool. "He said it was loose, so I told him how to wiggle it with his tongue and a second later, it just popped out! We almost lost it in the water." She sits on Lucy's lounger. Molly wasn't feeling great, so we agreed to take her to the pool with us. "Now the Tooth Fairy is gonna come."

"There is no Tooth Fairy," Trey says to her.

"Trey," Lucy says with her voice of warning.

I wait it out to see what Emelia might do.

"Yes, there is. She came for me last month when I lost my fourth tooth." Emelia opens her mouth and points at her bottom row of teeth where the tooth in question is missing.

"Well, she doesn't come for everyone." Trey's shoulders slump and a pang whooshes through my chest.

Emelia looks at me. I know Jed and Molly have had a conversation with her about how Trey has had a hard childhood and he hasn't received the same amount of love she's always been given. I'm not sure she understands fully, but she's always been understanding when Trey has an outburst.

"I'll prove it to you," she says with that same smug expression Jed gets when he's hell-bent on proving us wrong.

"How?" Trey asks, sulking.

"We'll have a sleepover and stay up all night until she comes. Then you'll see for yourself."

Lucy perks up from her investigation in the bushes. "Oh, you know she might not come if you're awake."

"We'll pretend to be asleep," Emelia says.

Worry etches on Lucy's features. How will we pull this off?

"I'm sure we can have a sleepover, but you'd have to ask your dad and mom," I say to my niece.

Emelia waves me off. "They'll say yes."

"Found it!" Lucy pops up with the tooth in her hand.

"Okay, let's figure out our plan." Emelia stands.

"Where are you going?" The desperation in Lucy's voice would give her away if they weren't seven-year-olds.

"To the pool. We can't tell the adults our plan." Emelia shakes her head and leads Trey back over to the shallow end of the pool.

"Oh my god, Adam?"

I nod, knowing we're in deep trouble. "We'll wait until they're asleep. They have to fall asleep at some point."

She quirks an eyebrow because every time the two of them have a sleepover, they're nightmares the next day because they actually can stay awake all night.

"What's your solution?" I ask.

She looks around the pool and sighs. "I think we need to find ourselves a Tooth Fairy."

Lucy sets her eyes on Chevelle, who looks none too pleased to be getting slathered in sunblock by our grandma. I quickly grab my phone off the small table by my lounger and snap a picture to preserve the moment for prosperity. Or for whenever I want to piss off my little sister by sending it to her.

"I don't think now is the time to ask," I say, knowing all too well how upset Chevelle is from having to be the grandmas' sidekick on this trip.

"It'll give her a reprieve." Lucy shifts to stand, and I follow because I don't think this will go well.

We wave at Emelia and Trey doing handstands in the water as we walk around the pool to Chevelle.

"What?" she asks, obviously irritated.

"Can we get you a drink?" I ask.

She points at both of us. "I see the look on your faces. Just tell me what you want."

"Who says we want something?" Lucy says, all sweet.

"We're going in for a dip. Want to join, Chevelle?" Dori sits up. "Oh, hey, you two."

We politely wave to Dori, Grandma, and Midge.

"I'm good, but thanks." She smiles at them, but the smile drops as soon as she turns back to us.

The three seniors get up and go, so Lucy and I sit on Grandma's lounger next to Chevelle.

"I swear you all owe me. Want to know what I had to do last night?" Chevelle starts right in as though she's been waiting all day for someone to vent to. "They put rollers in my hair. Those pink spongy things. And made me sleep in them."

Lucy smothers her laugh. "Your hair looks nice."

"It only looks nice because I jumped in the pool the minute I got down here this morning. Which upset them because I quote 'ruined the look.'" She shakes her head. "On top of that, Cam is telling every single guy here that we're dating, but keeping it from my family."

My head rears back. "Why would he do that?"

"He said all the guys want from me is sex."

I nod in agreement, and she throws up her hands.

"You guys have one minute to ask me whatever you came over here for."

I look at Lucy, and she nudges me to go. "Well, Trey lost his tooth today…"

Lucy shows it off like a prized possession.

"And?" Chevelle crosses her arms.

"And he doesn't believe in the Tooth Fairy, so Emelia put together this sleepover plan where they stay up all night and wait to catch the Tooth Fairy."

Chevelle's already shaking her head. "I'm not dressing up. Nope. I've already done enough by dealing with the grandmas nonstop for my entire vacation. Find someone else."

Just then, Cam saunters over, more tanned than I've ever seen him.

"This is only our second day. How are you so tan?" I ask.

"He fake baked at home," Chevelle says.

He looks at her in disgust. "I worked on the docks a lot this summer."

He slides Chevelle's legs to the side so he can sit on the end of her lounger, and she grunts. Those two haven't gotten along ever since Chevelle got older. They're always picking at each other.

"Here's your Tooth Fairy." She thumbs toward Cam.

"The Tooth Fairy is a woman," I say.

"Says who?" Chevelle sits up straight. "The Tooth Fairy could be a guy. Maybe the same guy who's ruined my vacation."

"What do you need?" Cam sips his drink, looking between Lucy and me.

"We need someone to dress up as the Tooth Fairy tonight to make Trey a believer," Lucy says.

Cam nods. "I'm in."

"What? Stop screwing around," Chevelle says.

Cam looks her straight in the eye. "I'll do it. I need a tutu, some glitter, and probably a headband or something."

Chevelle stares in disbelief that he agreed and isn't acting as if it's a huge ask.

I look at Lucy as if to say, *Are we really going to go with Cam?* But she knows as well as I do that there's a close to zero chance anyone else will agree.

"Then let's go shopping, Cam." Lucy stands.

"I'll help," Chevelle says, grabbing her stuff. "Adam, you're on kid and grandma patrol."

LATER THAT NIGHT, Cam waits in the hallway, dressed in his tutu and a sparkly T-shirt, with a wand and some sort of leg warmers. He has glitter in his hair, and they've drawn glittery stars on his face. I'll give it to the guy, he's definitely comfortable with himself. That T-shirt is stretched within an inch of its life because it's a woman's XL.

Lucy and I pretend to go to sleep while we hear giggles from Trey and Emelia. Trey is in his bed and Emelia is on the cot we had delivered to the room. The tooth is tucked under his pillow and Lucy is clutching my arm, waiting for it all to unfold.

Soon, Cam uses our key card and tiptoes in. He trips over a suitcase and curses under his breath, then apologizes. All I see is this plan becoming a dumpster fire.

But the giggling stops and the kids pretend they're sleeping. I watch Cam's silhouette in the dark, wondering how he's pulling this off.

"Be a good boy, Trey. I'll be saving your teeth. Here's a

little extra since I missed you a few times. It's been a busy couple of seasons," he whispers and leaves the dollar bill I gave him in place of the tooth.

Then Cam tiptoes out, tossing glitter all over the room as evidence he was there. That was not a part of the plan we discussed.

The minute the hotel room door closes, Trey jumps up and Emelia moves to his bed. "What did you get?"

Lucy and I pretend to be woken up, and Lucy turns on the light. "You two need to get to bed."

"You gotta be kidding me." Trey stares at the bill in his hand and I smile with pride that we pulled this off. "The Tooth Fairy is a dude, and he gave me a hundred-dollar bill."

Lucy and I both turn to one another with wide eyes. Lucy recovers faster than I do and gives Trey a huge hug. I ruffle his hair and tell him how awesome that is, then I sneak out into the hallway, following the glitter path all the way to the elevators.

Cam is standing there with Chevelle.

"That was really sweet," she says.

"Is all this glitter getting to me or did you just say something nice to me?" Cam asks.

"Cam!" I interrupt them, ignoring the look in my sister's eyes while she's looking at Cam. I don't like it. "You gave him a hundred dollars."

Chevelle's smile widens.

"He's had a rough life. The kid deserves it."

I shake my head. "That's what he's going to expect every time he loses a tooth now."

"Well, maybe you should be more careful when you're picking someone to play a supernatural creature next time." He winks.

I groan and walk back down the hall. Damn Cam.

I walk back into our hotel room and Trey's face is so full of happiness my heart could burst. The hundred dollars was worth it.

I can't believe I have Cam to thank for that. That guy surprises me more and more these days.

Chapter Six

Nikki

*D*ay three of our trip and I think maybe my teeth will be ground down to nubs by the time we leave. Noah sits in my lap, slapping at the water in the kiddie pool area, while I watch his father being accosted by a fan.

"Another one?" Posey sits next to me because Gavin is next to Logan, being accosted by the same fan. Obviously we have an MMA fighter/Hollywood celeb fan here.

We watch as the girl in the skimpiest bikini asks her friend to take a picture, then sandwiches herself between our men. We groan while they take the picture, and the girl looks at the phone and asks for another one. Of course, our men agree because it seems they quite like the attention.

They head to the bar after and the girl heads to the beach.

I look at Posey, who's interacting with Noah. "You better watch out. You're looking a little pink."

She presses a finger to her skin. "I'm good."

"It's hard to tell out here."

"Will you please not mother hen me?"

I roll my eyes and figure it's her problem if she spends the rest of her vacation in pain. She's a redhead. Of course she's going to burn.

"Look at Chevelle. What I wouldn't do for a body like

that," I say, completely jealous of her skimpy bikini that has less fabric than the onesie Noah wore on the way home from the hospital.

"I know, right?"

I glare at Posey. She looks practically the same. No baby bump yet, but she wears her bikini as well as ever.

Me, I'm in the water in my one-piece because of the stretch marks Noah gave me. Not that I'd trade the little guy for anything. "Talk to me after your stomach has blown up and shrunk down."

Her hand absently runs over her nonexistent belly. "It's weird. I barely remember I'm pregnant sometimes. No morning sickness or anything."

"Speaking of..."

Posey's already nodding. We're on the same wavelength because Molly has been very absent from our vacation, making the excuse that she thinks she has food poisoning. Right now, Jed's in the pool, throwing Emelia around, while Molly's on a lounge chair with a hat on and looking miserable.

"Something gives. She would've been right out there with them." Posey nods toward Jed and Emelia.

I nod. Molly's my best friend and she usually tells me everything, but ever since she got with Jed, I'm second in line. Which I understand, because I'm married. I get it. Most of the time.

"I say you go find out." Posey elbows me. "Want to go see Auntie?" Posey says to Noah, who shakes his head, his hands dipping into the water and splashing.

"What's up, ladies?" Gavin comes to Posey's side, handing her a fruity drink. "Virgin."

"How was the bar? Crowded?" Posey asks.

"Where's Logan?" I ask before he can respond.

"He got hung up at the bar with some fans. That man is a rock star down here."

"Tell me about it." We tried to go to dinner a couple nights ago because Mandi agreed to watch Noah and we had about five minutes of conversation without interruption. "Thank god we don't have to deal with this in Alaska."

"It's weird. I haven't been recognized in so long that it felt odd at first." Gavin runs his hand down his abs.

Posey stares at him. "Odd?"

He shrugs. "Yeah, but I'll admit, it felt nice."

Posey makes some noise and takes Noah from my lap, walking toward the middle of the kiddie pool.

"I suggest you go after her," I say to Gavin, who looks dumbfounded.

"Stone. Stone. Stone!" chanting comes from the outside bar.

I groan. Since Posey has Noah, I'm going to go drag my husband out of that tiki hut if it's the last thing I do.

I stomp over to the bar and stop when I see him posing for another damn picture, this time with two women on each side. Logan's all smiles until he looks beyond the camera and spots me. Since I have my hand on my cocked hip and impatience in my aura that he can feel all the way over there, he excuses himself and walks over to me.

"Hey, baby." He wraps his arm around my waist and kisses me on the lips. It's short and quick.

"Enjoying your fans?"

He nods. "Sorry, I tried to get away earlier, but then some guy got me talking about my fight with Miller and you know how I lose track of time sometimes when I reminisce."

"Listen, Logan, we've got two more days on this island, then we're going home to Alaska. I've spent the last three days watching you put your arm around every pretty woman in a bikini. Either you shut down your fans and spend some family time with us, or you can stay here while the rest of us return to Alaska." My voice is sugary sweet, topped with a dollop of threat.

Logan frowns and guilt washes over his face like the nearby ocean waves. "I'm sorry. I got carried away."

"Ya think?"

I know it was hard for Logan to retire. Although he enjoyed not being ridiculed and torn apart in the papers, he's missed people always knowing his name and throwing out the red carpet. If I'm honest, I forgot about his celebrity status until we landed in Hawaii and suddenly people were asking him if he's Logan Stone, the MMA fighter. Then add child star Gavin next to him, and I'm surprised we're not being chased by the paparazzi.

"Want me to watch Noah while you go to the spa?" he asks on our way back to the kiddie pool.

"No, I just want to spend time with you. I already don't feel like myself, having to wear this full-piece swimsuit."

He puts his hand on my arm. "Baby, you're the most gorgeous woman here."

I scoff and keep walking.

"I'm serious. And you could wear a bikini. You should wear the marks Noah gave you with pride."

"Come on, Logan, I don't want anyone to see those." They're fading, but they're still there.

"I want to kiss each and every one because they're proof of you giving us a healthy baby."

I cover my stomach even though the black Lycra swimsuit does it. "I just miss my old body."

He takes me in his arms and pulls me into his chest. "I don't. Not in the slightest. I like this one better and I'll like the next one after you have our second child even more."

I let my head fall to his chest. "I'm sorry for taking you away from your fans. I'm just feeling a little insecure these days."

His chest vibrates with amusement. "That's why you have me to give you the ego boosts you deserve." He holds me for a few more seconds. "Let's find a babysitter and have a night to ourselves."

I look up with my chin resting on his chest. "I'd love that."

He brushes away a stray tear with his thumb. "Me too."

LOGAN SWINDLED Posey into babysitting Noah. Said they could use the practice. The handoff didn't go smoothly though, because Noah was crying as though I was flying back to Alaska without him. Once we're back in our room, I change into sexy lingerie I brought just in case one of my siblings threw us a bone and babysat. After putting on a robe, I walk out of the bathroom to find a tray from room service.

"I'm only really hungry for one thing," I say, walking up to my husband at the edge of the bed.

He fiddles with the ties of my robe. "Me too. This is for after when we've worked up an appetite and are both starved." He nods at the cart.

My fingers run through his blond hair. "Always thinking ahead."

He unties my robe, and his hands slide along my waist until both cover my hips. His fingers dig in and he leans back to see my outfit. "I'm so sorry for what I did. I shouldn't have entertained any of those fans. You and Noah are my life. You're the only things that really matter to me."

I nod because I know that. I don't question it. And even if Noah is almost a year old and I'm still not happy with my body, I have to get more comfortable with the fact that I'll never have that perfectly flawless, flat stomach again.

"I know. I get it. You never want to disappoint anyone."

He rests his chin on my chest and stares up at me. "I never want to disappoint you or Noah."

I straddle his lap and bend down to kiss him. "You'd never disappoint us. Ever."

His hands slide around until he grabs each ass cheek. "I like this lingerie."

"I'm glad you like it."

His head falls into the crook of my neck, and he places light kisses there, up to my earlobe and across my jaw. It doesn't take long for things to heat up. After all, sex isn't on the table as much as it used to be before Noah was born.

Logan strips off my robe and his hungry gaze soaks me in, causing my heart to kick-start. This man is gorgeous and he's all mine.

I'm on my back and his fingers are hooked into the sides of my panties when there's a knock on the door. Worse, I hear Noah wailing in the hall.

Logan looks up at me. "Ignore it?"

He chuckles and I swat him. Both of us climb off the bed and I hurriedly pull the robe back on. We open the door to find Gavin standing there with a very upset Noah, reaching for me the minute he sees me.

"Oh, sweet boy," I say, running my hand down Noah's back.

"Sorry, guys, I tried. Posey's burned and miserable. Noah never really calmed down, and without Posey's help, I'm pretty helpless, which probably means I'm gonna be a horrible father." He pushes a hand through his hair and cringes.

"No, you won't," Logan tells him.

"I couldn't even keep him occupied so you two could have sex."

I laugh and take Noah into the room. He's a sweaty, crying mess. His bottom lip quivers as he rests his head on my shoulder, and I rub his back. The mom guilt kicks in immediately. I shouldn't have left him. He's going to have nightmares about this for years.

Logan says goodbye to Gavin and joins me, lifting the lids off the room service plates. "At least we can eat."

I spoon up a small piece of the cake and allow Noah to taste it, which perks him up. Logan cuts up the steak and shrimp and feeds me my meal. I smile at him.

"What?" he says. "I know. Sorry it didn't work out tonight."

I shake my head. "No, I'm happy. The happiest I've ever been."

"Baby, our whole night blew up."

"No, we're all together and that's all that matters." I give Noah a little more cake, and Logan makes his bottle once he's calmed down.

As we sit up with our backs against the headboard and our baby between us, sucking on his bottle, I'm more thankful than ever for what I have.

The next day, I go down to the gift shop early, buy a bikini, and wear it at the pool all day.

Logan can't take his eyes off me and never leaves my side. "I want every guy to know you're taken."

Luckiest woman in the world.

Chapter Seven

Posey

"**C**an you please lie somewhere else?" I know there's a bite to my tone as I try to lie in the king-size bed. Poor Gavin is doing everything he can to help me and I'm still complaining. But I'm so uncomfortable and I feel terrible that I let my sister down and had to send Noah back. "And put some aloe on me."

"Well, I'd have to touch you to put it on."

The room is dark except for the glow of the television and there's no sound because I said he had it on too loud five minutes ago.

"I'm so sorry. I'm being a complete bitch, but it hurts sooo bad."

The bed dips and I cringe. "I know, but you have to let me put on this aloe. It'll help your skin. Hopefully by tomorrow you'll feel a lot better."

"I ruined our whole vacation." Tears spring in my eyes but I don't want them to fall for fear the tear tracks will feel like lines of fire down my face. The shower was like a million needles pricking me at once.

"You didn't ruin our vacation. Let's just get through tonight."

I sniffle all the snot that wants to come out now that I'm a complete mess. "Are you sure you want to marry me? I wouldn't want to marry me. And I'm having your kid. If I can't survive a sunburn, how am I going to survive childbirth?" I look up at his dark silhouette. "We're doomed."

He laughs and shakes his head. "I love your imagination. Now where is that fighter who competed against me the entire mayoral race?"

"She's dead. Her body feels like she's been baked in an oven then put in the dryer."

"Cute visual."

I hear the bottle being opened and brace my entire body, closing my eyes, but nothing happens. "Gav?"

"I'm not going to surprise you. Are you ready?"

I nod and stiffen, waiting for him to put the aloe on my skin. He goes to the tops of my feet first, which aren't as bad since my lower half was in the water.

"Do you think I harmed the baby?"

"We called the doctor, remember? She said no."

"But... maybe Dr. Bailey is lying to make us feel good. To make me not feel like a shitty mother. I could've at least worn a one-piece," I wail.

Gavin rubs the aloe over my body. "All this energy you're putting into beating yourself up isn't good. The baby is fine. You're going to be fine. Everything will be fine."

I say nothing because we're going to have to disagree on this one.

After he's done applying the lotion, I just lie there on the bed naked, not wanting to move a muscle for fear of it hurting. All the while, my mind works like crazy, thinking I harmed the baby, knowing for sure I harmed my skin. I'm fair skinned—what was I thinking? I'm sure Mandi's still all porcelain beautiful since she lathered on sunscreen all day.

The bed dips again, and I refrain from complaining because Gavin is probably ready to walk out that door. He situates himself so his back rests on the headboard and puts a pillow on his lap.

"Tell me something embarrassing."

"What?" I shake my head.

"Come on. We need to pass the time. I'll tell you mine first if you want."

"Okay then. You go first."

He blows out a breath. "Okay, when I was on *The Carters*, we had a live audience, so we didn't always get a lot of breaks. I forgot to go to the bathroom one time before coming to set, and as the scene continued, the urge grew stronger but there was nothing I could do. I ended up pissing my pants and the director finally yelled cut. The audience laughed because I think they thought it was written into the script, but it wasn't."

"You were little."

"I worried for months that one of those people was going to tell someone or a picture would end up in a magazine or something. My older siblings from the family all made it a running joke and the director never said action again until she'd asked me if I'd gone to the bathroom."

I giggle and my face cracks. "Ouch."

"Serves you right." He laughs at himself. "Want to move onto the pillow?"

It looks as if it's a mile away, but I slide my body along the soft sheets and lay my head on the pillow in his lap. He pulls my hair out from under me, sprawling it out over the pillow and running his fingers through it in a soothing motion.

"Now it's your turn," he says.

"I've never been someone who gets easily embarrassed in front of others. But I did do something you might think is funny."

"What?" There's a smile in his voice.

"When I was younger and you were on *Briarwood Academy*, I may have written a fanfic and made myself your girlfriend."

He laughs. "You did?"

"Yeah," I say meekly. "Kind of stupid, right?"

"I'm both honored and impressed."

Maybe I was wrong, and I do embarrass easily. Or maybe it's all part of admitting to your fiancé exactly how much of a fangirl you were for him when he was a child star. "I'm mortified." I wouldn't have thought it possible, but my cheeks get even hotter than they already are.

"I wish I'd known you back then. You would've made it more bearable if you'd played my girlfriend for real."

I look up, and the glow of the television reflects the love swimming in his eyes. "Me too."

"Now, when can I get my hands on this fanfic?"

"Uh, never."

"If you weren't sunburned right now, I would tickle the information out of you."

"And I wish you could tickle me."

He doesn't give me too much grief about the fanfic thing —mostly because I don't think he likes to talk about his acting days. But he asks me questions about my first memory, and whether I think our baby will be a boy or a girl, then we go back and forth on names. During the conversation, I grow sleepy, and eventually everything goes black.

WE HAVE two days left at the resort, so the next morning, we eat breakfast and I venture out under a tree. Luckily, last night did me good and I'm feeling a lot better, but my skin won't be seeing the sun until we're back in Alaska.

Chevelle comes over to me under the tree. "I can't take it anymore! I'll pay you to switch rooms. You and Gavin aren't doing it anyway with you looking like a hairless cat."

"Chevelle!"

"Sorry, I'm just annoyed. I thought I was going to get laid this trip, then Cam plays that stupid stunt. And I get stuck with the grandmas who constantly want to be in bed early. But there's a beauty regimen they do that takes an hour. An hour, Posey! And it involves cold cream." I laugh and she narrows her eyes at me. "Last night, they were talking about having sex and how I should go after Cam because he looks like someone with endurance."

"Ew!" My face twists in distaste.

"Exactly. Someone needs to help me. Seriously!"

"Ask Mandi or Clara, I'm sure they'll trade. It's only two more nights."

"I already asked. Those two are thick as thieves this trip. They hang out by the beach instead of the pool. Mandi said she's always on Grandma Ethel duty and it's my turn."

I can't blame Mandi. She's right. She's always the one making sure Grandma Ethel gets where she needs to while Chevelle and I play the baby of the family card and don't get called to do much for Grandma.

Gavin brings me a drink. "Do you want something, Chevelle?"

She shakes her head. "No, I just need to figure out how the hell I can get into someone else's room. See you two later."

She stands and waves, walking away with her perfectly tanned skin in a skimpy bikini that only accentuates her curves. I'm jealous.

We sip our drinks. "Thanks for last night," I say to Gavin.

"I'd put my arm around your shoulders, but I'm afraid to hurt you. I can't wait until you're healed." He leans forward and places the gentlest kiss on my lips.

"Me too."

"We'll have other vacations."

"I know, but this is probably the last one before the baby. I see how it changed Nikki and Logan and I don't want it to change us."

We look across the pool where Noah is engaged with Emelia and Trey while Logan keeps touching Nikki.

"They don't look unhappy to me," he says.

"No. No, they don't." I smile and bring my fruity drink to my lips. The coolness feels good. "You're the best."

He pretends to be smug but ends up laughing. "I try."

"I love you," I whisper and lean my head on his shoulder.

"I love you more," he whispers back.

We had a few good days, and I know from experience this sunburn won't last forever. I really hope our little one gets their daddy's skin tone though.

Chapter Eight

Chevelle

After a night of discussing hairstyles—in which each grandma gave me their opinion on what I should do with my hair—the magic time of seven o'clock rolls around and we must all prepare for bed unless we want to turn into pumpkins. When I asked why they don't go to bed this early in Alaska, they told me there must be something about the tropical air that tires them out.

So I watch Grandma do her nightly routine of face washing and cream, then she slides into bed. I lie down under the covers and stare at the ceiling. Eight o'clock bedtime. On vacation. In Hawaii.

Then Midge's C-pap machine starts up in the room next door and I can hear it because we must keep the adjoining door open. When I suggested closing it on the first night, all three informed me that we couldn't do that because what would happen if someone sneaked into their room and we didn't hear? We couldn't do anything to help them anyway and vice versa.

Grandma Ethel's light snores join the C-pap machine, then Dori mumbles something about donuts and not getting there in time.

I continue to lie there, restless and annoyed.

Screw this.

I slowly get out of bed, grab my cell phone and key, and tiptoe across the room. Ever so gently, I pry the door open and slide through the smallest sliver. I wait for a moment to see if I've woken anyone, but their trio of sounds is going strong.

Once I shut the door as quietly as I can, I hightail it to the elevator. Someone is looking out for me because the elevator doors ding open as soon as I press the button and my escape is complete. I head to the other room and knock on the door of the only person I know who has extra space.

Unfortunately, as soon as Cam opens the door, I second-guess myself for a moment—until I picture myself lying there waiting to fall asleep for hours, listening to the three of them. I push through his open door.

"I can't do it anymore. I'm staying here, and I don't want to hear boo about it." I stop in my tracks as soon as I'm inside. "A suite? You've had a suite this whole time and I'm staying with three senior citizens?"

He chuckles and walks back over to the couch where the television has on some baseball game. "I didn't think you'd want to stay with me."

"But we're dating, remember?" I roll my eyes and plop down next to him. "And you face the ocean? What it must be like to be you." I stand and head over to the windows. Or should I say the sliding doors that open to a spacious balcony? "You have a nicer room than the two famous guys here."

He follows me out. "Beautiful, right?"

I nod, watching some couple walking down the sand, hand in hand. I haven't been up at this time of night since I got here and it's gorgeous. The sun has already set, but the sky is still lit up in oranges, yellows, and pinks. "You have this view and you're watching baseball."

He chuckles and sips his beer. "Want a drink?"

I turn to follow him to the mini-fridge. "Why are you in your room?"

"Because everybody I'm here with is in their room already."

"But that doesn't stop you from going down to the bar and picking up someone." I accept the beer from him and head back out to the patio to watch the colors before they disappear into darkness.

He shrugs, taking the chair next to me. "I'm not really into it."

"You not into hooking up?" I touch his forehead. "You sure you're feeling okay?"

He shakes his head. "Don't give me that shit. You know I don't sleep around."

"Anymore." I raise my beer. "Back in the day, you loved those tourists."

"Now I'm more into townies." He winks.

"Clearly, since you had to make up a fake relationship with me."

He takes a long pull of his beer. "You're lucky I didn't make a public spectacle of us."

"You mean yourself."

"You're my girlfriend, so…"

We watch the sky in silence after that, and I'm in awe, although I wish I were out on the beach.

"Next time, I want to watch this from the sand," I say, rising from my chair to go back inside. "I'm starved. Why don't we order food, money bags?"

"I'm not money bags." You'd think I'd called him some nasty name from his tone, which is odd because Cam is rarely ever offended. He tosses me the room service menu.

"I'll gladly take you out though. Want to go to some hot spots on the island?"

"I'd love to, but I'm in my pajamas." I look down at my tank top and shorts.

He looks at the time on his phone. "We have about five minutes. Money bags can buy you something from the gift shop."

"Seriously? How do you know when it closes?"

"My family comes every year. Who do you think gave Marla and Hank the location to plan this little vacation?"

I bite my lip. I want to go out. Lord knows I could use a little bit of fun, but I'm wondering if we should invite Mandi and Clara. But I really like the spontaneity of this. "I'm in."

He swipes his keys and wallet off the dresser. "Let's go."

Cam is a man of his word. We go down to the gift shop, and I grab a sundress, sandals, and a scrunchie to pull back my hair.

"I have no license or money."

He tips the doorman, who whistles for a taxi. "Tonight's on me. Just... no arguing, okay?"

"But that's what we do best." I elbow him in the ribs.

"Not tonight. Tonight is only for fun."

We climb into the taxi, and it suddenly feels awkward being alone with Cam. Especially since we're going out by ourselves. We've never done that before. One of my siblings is always around to act as a buffer.

The first stop is a bar and restaurant on the beach. Cam orders all the appetizers on the menu while I'm in the bathroom, and there's a fruity drink waiting for me when I return. He's still drinking beer.

"Too girly for you?" I take the long toothpick with the strawberry, kiwi, and orange on it, biting off the fruit.

He takes my wrist and directs my hand to his mouth,

then he bites off the orange. A second later, he's chewing and spitting out the rind.

"Show-off," I say, enjoying the strawberry.

We talk about nothing of importance. The trip, Posey's sunburn, Logan and Gavin's fangirls, the fact that Jed and Molly are barely out of their room, and lastly, I tell him about my time with the grandma gang. Before I know it, the appetizers are practically gone and I'm on my third drink.

Now this is vacation.

"Nightclub?" He raises an eyebrow in question.

"Are you really asking me if I want to go dance?" No man has ever willingly wanted to go to a dance club with me.

"One rule." He holds up his finger.

"What?"

"We're not picking up. You dance with me at all times."

I laugh, finishing my drink. "You know you can stop the whole protective act, right? We aren't with my brothers, and they wouldn't care if I picked someone up tonight anyway."

He shakes his head. "If you think that, then you don't know your brothers. I'll gladly bill you for half of tonight, we can go back to the hotel, and you can go sleep with the grandmas."

He makes it sound as enticing as sleeping in a lion's den.

"Fine." I groan because what am I going to do, pick up a man and take him to Cam's hotel room? And I'm certainly not going with some stranger to another hotel.

With a satisfied smile, Cam raises his hand for the check.

***

THREE HOURS later and I'm sober because Cam actually enjoys dancing. I didn't know that fun fact about him. I thought he was just a really good wedding dancer, but it turns out he has fun. We danced all night, rarely drank except for bottles of water because of how much we were sweating, and now we're walking into the hotel looking like drunk tourists even though we're completely sober.

I stop in my tracks when I see Fisher walking one of the twins around the lobby. We don't have enough time to hide before he turns around and spots us.

Both his eyebrows rise. "You two were out? Together?" His mouth presses into a tight line.

Cam casually shoves his hands in his pockets as if that's some bro signal that he didn't touch me all night. When in fact, there were times on the dance floor I wondered what it would feel like if he did. Just the accidental brush of his finger on my skin sent scorching heat to my center. I know he felt it too because his eyes looked as starved as I felt.

"We hit up a nightclub. Chevelle's been holed up with the grandmas. She deserved it." Cam breaks the distance, his gait so nonchalant he deserves an Oscar. "Who's up?" He peeks around to get a look at the baby's face.

"Laurie, of course. She's hardly slept since we got here."

I peek my head around too and see that she's completely out.

"The minute we put her down or she's not in our arms, it's game over. I'm trying to let Allie and Axel sleep." He looks at us. "You both reek. Go take a shower. Good luck sneaking back into the room," he says to me.

I nod because it's easier just not telling him I'm sleeping in Cam's room.

Cam must agree because he slaps my brother on my back. "See you tomorrow. Try to get some sleep."

Fisher nods and walks the other way, rocking Laurie the whole time.

We go to the elevator bank and press the button frantically as if we got caught doing something wrong.

Once we're back in his room, Cam offers me the shower first. I go into the bathroom, feeling all hot and bothered for Cameron Baker and wishing he were in here with me. What is wrong with me? This cannot be happening.

I strip off my clothes and take a shower, using the shampoo and body wash I immediately know that Cam must've brought with him because it smells just like him. Which does nothing to ease the need that's been building inside me all night. I lotion up my body, and once I'm done, I realize my pajamas are in the main area of the suite. So I wrap a towel around myself and peek out. There's no sign of Cam, so I step out, but he comes out of the bedroom at that exact moment and we run into each other.

My towel slips, he grabs my arms to steady me, and the towel falls to the floor. We both stand there in shock for a moment, me completely naked and him wearing only shorts. We stare into one another's eyes before I shake my head and fumble to grab my towel.

"I'm so sorry," I mumble. "My pajamas..."

"Yeah, I'm just going to." He thumbs toward the bathroom. "Yeah... okay."

The door shuts and I let out the biggest sigh. Now I just need to get through tonight.

Chapter Nine

Jed

This is the vacation from hell. Here I thought we would have a fun time with Emelia, but she's probably spent more time with only me or with Adam and Lucy than with Molly and me together.

"Mommy's sick again?" Emelia asks as we hear Molly throwing up in the toilet.

"Yeah, I think she caught a bug." I ruffle her hair.

"If you catch a bug, you throw up?" She shakes her head. "No more fireflies."

I chuckle and put out her swimsuit for her to change into. It's our last day here and we fly home later today, which I personally cannot wait for. "No, bug means a stomach bug, a virus. Like when you had the flu last year?"

I swear every muscle in her face falls. "That's how Mommy feels?"

I nod. Probably worse, since she's felt like shit longer than Emelia did. I'm half tempted to take her to the emergency room, but she promised me she's okay.

"Poor Mommy." She changes into her swimsuit and sits on the bed. "How do we make her feel better? I took medicine. We can give her medicine."

"We've tried and not much is helping her. But we'll keep trying." I give Emelia a smile I hope is reassuring.

She nods a bunch of times. "I have a secret." She leans in and I bend down for her to whisper it in my ear. "The Tooth Fairy isn't a girl, it's a boy."

I try not to laugh. Adam and Lucy told me what Cam did for Trey. "How do you know?" I whisper back conspiratorially.

She makes a motion of zipping her lips.

"You're not going to tell me?"

"Nope." She laughs as I tickle her. "Daddy! Daddy!"

The bathroom door opens, and I let Emelia go. We both look at Molly as she comes out, pale as a ghost.

Emelia jumps off the bed. "You need the doctor, Mommy."

Molly pushes her hand through Emelia's dark hair. "Not yet. Are you going to the pool?"

"Last day?" I say as if I know what to do. She's spent the majority of her time either in this room on the bathroom floor or on a lounge chair with a hat so low it covers her eyes.

She nods. "I need to… um…" She looks at Emelia. "Trey already down there?"

"Let me see!" Emelia runs to the window that looks at the pool. We sure got lucky to get this ground-floor room. Not. "Yep! He's there." She runs to grab her flip-flops and goggles. "Can I go?"

Molly shoots me the look that says she needs something but doesn't want to discuss it in front of little ears.

"I'll take her quick and be right back up."

Molly nods and holds out her arms. Emelia runs into them. "Have fun. I'm sorry I'm not much fun on this trip."

Emelia pulls back from Molly. "It's okay. You're sick. I understand."

Molly smiles. "Thanks, kiddo." I go to kiss her, but she puts her hand over my mouth. "Nope."

"Okay."

We leave and Emelia runs down the hall, knowing the way to the pool by now. I follow, and I know she stops when she's out of my eyesight. It's our rule and she knows it.

"Hurry, Daddy!"

We walk outside. Sure enough, most of my family is there, soaking up the last moments of our last day.

"You seen Chevelle?" Adam asks as soon as I approach their chairs to ask them to watch Emelia once again.

"Can I go in, Daddy? Can I?" Emelia flings off her flip-flops, one hitting Lucy in the head. "Sorry, Auntie Lucy."

"Emelia, you have to watch what you're doing," I say.

Lucy rubs her head. "It's okay."

"Go." I look at Emelia and nod toward the pool.

She runs and jumps into the water where Trey is. Then they talk about their nights. Poor Emelia only has stories of trying to watch a movie while Molly threw up dinner.

"Chevelle?" I ask, coming back to the conversation.

"Yeah. I guess Grandma woke up and she wasn't in her bed. And she's not out here yet."

I frown then shrug. "She's an adult. I'm sure she's fine. Probably on some long walk as a means of escape."

Adam doesn't seem overly concerned. "I guess."

"Do you mind watching Emelia again?" I run a hand through my hair.

"Molly still sick?" Lucy asks.

I nod.

Adam looks back at his wife, and they share a look. "Have you thought maybe..."

My forehead wrinkles. "What?"

"She's throwing up everything she eats. She's tired..."

Lucy waves her hand as though she's trying to get me to figure out her thoughts.

"Pregnant? Could she be pregnant?" Adam blurts.

Of course these two would know what signs to look for. They're trying to have a baby of their own while fostering.

"Um..." I think about it for a second. The thought never even crossed my mind. "I don't think so. We never talked about it or made any decisions about having a baby."

Adam laughs and glances at Lucy as if I'm a funny guy. It agitates me. "You don't have to decide you want a baby for it to happen."

"I know, dumbass." I head to the pool's edge. "Emelia, listen to Uncle Adam and Aunt Lucy, okay?"

She nods and puts up her hand in an okay gesture. "Gotcha. Take care of Mommy," she says and swims off.

Leaving the music and people having fun, I go back inside, wishing Molly could've enjoyed at least five minutes of this.

I walk by the gift shop and pause. What if Adam and Lucy are right?

"Fuck it," I murmur and head inside, looking near the condoms.

Sure enough, there's a pregnancy test. Only one kind, but I grab two just in case. The woman smiles as she rings me up and glances at my left hand when I hand her some cash. She looks as though she was about to say something but stops when she sees I'm not wearing a wedding ring. I frown and take my change and the bag, annoyed. I love Molly more than some husbands, but I bet if I had a wedding band on my hand, the clerk would be all smiles.

I'm heading back to my room when I pass the elevators. I wish we could've been on a higher floor, but maybe next time. The elevator doors open and Cam and Chevelle stand inside.

"Hey, people are looking for you." I point at Chevelle and continue walking until I step back and do a double take because they both have a look on their faces that I recognize from my time sneaking around with Molly. Like they've been caught. "What's going on?"

"Nothing." Cam steps away from Chevelle.

Chevelle doesn't have any smart-ass remark. She just walks out of the elevator. "I got locked out. My key card isn't working." She heads off toward the front desk.

Cam follows me and I look at him once I'm at my room. I motion to the door. "This is me."

"Oh yeah, see you later," he says and continues walking.

I watch him for a moment, and he walks by the pool door, glances over his shoulder to see me still there, and continues walking again. I don't even want to know. I have enough shit to deal with right now. When I enter the room, Molly's putting on her swimsuit.

"What are you doing?"

"It's our last day. I'm going to suck this up. Just throw up in the pool if I have to and apologize for embarrassing your entire family." She's practically out of breath from just standing and dressing.

"Sit down." I point at the bed.

She eyes the bag in my hand. "What's that?"

"You wanted to talk to me about something without Emelia around, right?" I sit down next to her on the edge of the bed.

She nods. "I'm a tad worried this might not be a stomach bug."

"Why?"

"I haven't had a fever. I can't keep anything down after I eat."

I open the bag from the store and hand her a pregnancy test.

Her eyes widen. "You think so too?"

"I didn't until Adam and Lucy asked." To my knowledge, we were being careful.

"We only use condoms, did one rip or something?"

I shrug. "Truthfully, I'm not religious in checking them. I mean, we're together and I know we've discussed adding to our family, so…"

"So you'd be okay with this?" She looks down at her stomach.

"Yeah, of course. I love watching you with Emelia, and I missed so much of her growing up. I want to experience that with you. Us raising our kid together, Emelia being an older sister. I'd be more than okay with it."

She smiles and holds up the test. "Then I guess we only have one thing to do."

I follow her into the bathroom and sit on the floor while she pees on the stick. When you have a seven-year-old, the whole privacy in the bathroom thing goes out the window. She finishes, washes her hands, and joins me on the floor.

"Not sure what we'll do if you're this sick through the whole pregnancy."

"God, I hope not." Her hand takes mine, and I squeeze it as I use my free hand to set the timer on my phone.

Neither of us says much while we wait. I'm guessing we're both lost in our thoughts about what comes with a new baby. But I meant what I said to her—I'd love to have a baby. We're lifers. She's stuck with me, married or not.

The buzzer goes off on my phone, and she picks up the test off the floor. "Ready?"

"Ready," I say, giving her hand one more squeeze.

She looks down and tears fill her eyes. She nods. "I'm pregnant."

I place my hand on her stomach. "We're pregnant."

"Then can you take throw-up duty now?"

We laugh, and I pull her into my chest. "I can't wait to see your belly swollen with my baby," I murmur in her ear.

She stands and takes my hand, but then she grows pale again and puts up her finger. With her head in the toilet, she loses the rest of her breakfast. I really hope this sickness is short lived because I'm not sure I can bear to see her this miserable for nine months.

Chapter Ten

Cam

We reach the airport, and everyone is still hounding Chevelle about where she slept last night. She's going with the story that she slept in her room and sneaked out early for a walk on the beach, then got breakfast and enjoyed some Chevelle time.

In reality, we woke up late and everyone was up by the time we figured out her key card didn't work. Apparently Grandma Ethel thought she'd been abducted and didn't want anyone to get into the room. I think Ethel just wanted to catch Chevelle in whatever she thought she was up to.

The airport is a zoo when we walk in. A lot of people looked pissed off, and I see that there are a few canceled flights on the board. By the time we get to our ticket agent, the woman looks as if she's about a minute away from quitting.

"The plane has been overbooked, so we're asking for volunteers to take a layover in San Francisco for the night, then fly out tomorrow morning to Anchorage. As a thank you, we'll offer you a credit to your account with the airline."

We all look at one another.

Clara is the first one to speak up. "I need to get home."

"How many seats do you have left?" Jed asks.

"Thirteen," she says. "And honestly, I need to assign names immediately for those seats."

Jed turns around. "I gotta get Molly home, guys. I don't want to be an asshole but..."

Everyone nods, understanding—she's been sick the entire trip.

"I hate to be a bitch, but I think those of us with kids should take the direct flight," Nikki says.

Clara groans but nods. It's understandable.

"I mean, it's hard traveling, and to take them to San Fran and then get on another flight in the morning," Nikki continues. I know she hates acting as though she's more important than others.

"No, Nikki, you're right," Mandi says.

"So?" the agent asks.

Jed starts getting everyone's driver's licenses and their luggage for those getting on the direct flight.

"We've got a night in San Francisco." I pull out my phone and send a text to Xavier, telling him to free up his schedule.

"We have the grandmas," Mandi says.

"I'm not sharing a room with them at the hotel," I say. "They'll have to share a bed."

"They can have one room, us three girls can have one room, and Cam?" Mandi looks at me expectantly.

I pick up the phone. "I'll go make the reservations now."

I walk away to call a few hotels I've stayed at when we go to visit Xavier, then I get a text from him.

Who is we?

Your family, jackass. And me and Clara.

K. I'll be at The Thirsty Monk tonight.

> Don't sound too excited.

The three dots appear then disappear, and no other text comes through.

After I call two hotels, I'm able to get us all at the same one, which will make it easier when we leave tomorrow morning. I head back over to the group of three women and three seniors. Great, six women and me. And not at all in the way I ever envisioned in my dreams.

We all get booked for our two flights, and after making it through security—where we all razzed Fisher about being a pain in the ass again—we go our separate ways. Everyone with kids heads to their plane, and all us singletons go in another direction.

TALK ABOUT DRAINING. Getting six women, three of whom are elderly, to the baggage claim and then to the arrivals area to grab taxis is no easy feat. I feel as if I ran a marathon. Somehow, we make it, but I'm ushered by Mandi into the car with the grandmas in case we get separated. For someone who is used to taking care of the grandmas, she's sure gotten good at passing the responsibility over.

"Where are you going tonight?" Dori asks.

"Just a place Xavier told me about."

"Oh, do they have beer?" Midge asks.

"I'm pretty sure," I say.

"Then we're in."

I glance at the clock on the taxi's dash. "It's past your bedtime."

"We do not have bedtimes. Sure, we like to go to bed by

eight, but we can stay out too." Ethel looks as if she's ready to throw down. "Plus, I want to see my grandson."

"This is the football player?" Midge asks.

The taxi driver glances at us.

"Xavier Greene," I say. "You're driving his grandma right now."

The taxi driver looks impressed. It's odd to me, since I still think of Xavier as the little brother of my best friend. The kid who always whined when he couldn't play quarterback. Now we're passing fucking billboards with his picture on them.

We pull up to the hotel and I check everyone in on my dime because there's no way I was staying at that shit airport hotel the airline was only willing to pay for. Not that I care. The Greenes have done more than enough for me over the years.

"Another suite?" Chevelle asks when I hand out the key cards.

"How do you know he had a suite?" Clara asks, her forehead creased.

Chevelle turns beet red, and I love that she outed herself. "He was bragging. You know Cam." She rolls her eyes, and I chuckle inwardly.

On the way to the elevator, I fill them in on our plans. "So, everyone changes, we meet down here in a half hour, and we'll head to The Thirsty Monk."

"Why there?" Mandi asks.

"I messaged Xavier and that's where he is."

Clara's head whips in my direction. "We weren't going to message him."

I know she and Xavier have had their problems, but we're in his town.

"We can't come to San Fran and not see Xavier."

"Yes, we can, and in fact, we planned on it." Chevelle puts her arm around Clara's shoulders.

"Well fuck, no one told me," I say, throwing my hands in the air. "I'll just go by myself then."

"It's too late now. We all have to go, otherwise we look like assholes." Mandi shakes her head, and they file into the elevator, pressing the button before I can step in. "Get the next one, Cam."

Jesus. "How was I supposed to know?" I mumble to myself, waiting for their elevator to go up so I can press the button for another one.

The entire time I'm getting settled in my room, I try to think of a way to get out of this. Say our plane detoured somewhere? But knowing those girls, one of them has posted their location on social media. And I don't want to lie to Xavier. Plus, if Fish calls him at some point, he's sure to mention we were here, then I look like the asshole.

I chalk the girls' reaction up to female hormones and jump in the shower.

A half hour later, I'm alone in the lobby.

Forty-five minutes later, I'm still alone in the lobby.

An hour later, the grandma gang shows up looking not much different than they did earlier.

"Sorry, Cam, we fell asleep," Ethel says.

"Power nap for your big night out, I get it," I joke, but none of them seem to like my humor. I'm really scoring zero for two tonight.

It takes an hour and fifteen minutes and a million texts from Ethel and me before the girls come down. I'm not sure where they think we're going, but they're all done up in full faces of makeup. Mandi's wearing jeans, a blouse, and heels. Chevelle must have loaned Clara one of her dresses because it's skintight, while Chevelle's is more like a Clara dress, conservative and not Chevelle's style at all. That doesn't mean I can't help picturing what she looks like underneath it. Not after last night anyway.

"Could you take any longer?" I grumble, standing to go out the lobby doors.

"Yes, we could have." Clearly Chevelle is back to her snarky self.

"We're going to walk if everyone's okay with that?" I ask, not wanting to flag down another two cars.

"My bunions, so not too far. Otherwise, you'll have to carry me," Midge says, smiling at me.

I feign a smile. "Okay, right."

The Thirsty Monk is only two blocks away, and when we walk in, I see a lot of Xavier's teammates. They're taking a spot on the far right and Xavier must sense us because he turns to face us. He doesn't smile right away, but his eyes zero in on Clara.

I can feel the tension between them. Whatever happened is still tearing them apart.

"Come on. Let's get a drink." Mandi guides Clara to the bar.

The rest of us break the distance, although I'm not sure Xavier knows we're here because he's still watching Clara.

Ethel takes Xavier's face between her thumb and forefinger, pulling him down to place a kiss on his cheek. "What? No hug for your grandma?"

He quickly bends down and hugs his grandma, then makes the rounds through the other two grandmas and Chevelle.

"Did you loan her a dress?" is the first question he asks his stepsister.

Chevelle stares at him long and hard. "Yeah, and I think she's a knockout in it."

He doesn't say anything, and I put my hand out between us. "What's up, man?"

Xavier shakes my hand and we give one another a man hug, but his sole attention is on Clara.

"Shit, is that you, Cam?" Ben, one of his teammates, comes over. "Damn, I didn't know you were in town." I do the whole man hug thing with him, and he stares over my shoulder. "Is that Clara?"

Ben looks at Xavier, and I wonder how much he's told him, but I'm shocked when Ben leaves all of us and puts his arm around Clara's shoulder, saying hello. Chevelle looks at me, and Xavier's Adam's apple bobs.

"Come sit," Xavier finally says. "What do you want to drink, Grandma, Dori, Midge?"

Just like that, he avoids dealing with whatever we're all missing here. Even I know he won't always be able to hide out here in San Francisco. He'll return home and have to face Clara and deal with whatever went down between them. They were way too good of friends for it all to just get thrown in the dumpster and lit on fire.

Chapter Eleven

Clara

I look ridiculous in Chevelle's dress. This isn't me. Not by a long shot.

We're not at the bar for five minutes before Ben finds me. He puts his arm around my shoulders.

"So, do blondes have more fun?" he says, making fun of the fact the first time he met me, I was a brunette.

He's a nice enough guy. Definitely makes it clear that he likes me, which is a plus, obviously.

"I think redheads have the most fun," Mandi says, and I shoot her a thank-you look while the bartender brings us the drinks we ordered.

"Put those on my tab," Ben says, picking up my drink and leading me over to the table.

"No worries, I got my own," Mandi grumbles and follows us.

"Sorry, let me introduce you to some of our teammates you might not have met yet." Ben leads me right into the middle of all the guys.

Mandi stops and says hello to Xavier, and if I don't do the same, I'll be the petty one. So I take my drink from Ben and walk over to Xavier. He's already staring at me, so he straightens when I approach.

"Hey, Clara," he says. "You look great."

I sip my drink, so the fact we're not hugging isn't awkward. I've been to this bar with him many times before when I'd visit. I manage to put on a smile. "You too. Where's Giulia?"

"We broke up. While I was at home with Dad this summer."

Guess the gossip blogs got something right for once.

"I'm sorry," I say, not really sorry at all.

"Thanks."

I nod and sip my drink, unsure what else to say.

"How was Hawaii?" he asks.

Ethel goes into detail, talking about all the fun she had with Chevelle and how she wants to plan a girls' trip sometime. She assures me I'll be invited, but who are we kidding? I'm not really part of the Greene clan anymore. My friendship with Xavier kept me there and now my sister is married to one, so that pulls me in on some occasions, but this was my last vacation with them. It's just too awkward with what happened between Xavier and me.

"Come play some darts with me." Ben doesn't really ask as he drags me over. But he's a welcome distraction from Xavier and our history.

So I play with him and another couple, and when we're done that round, another one of Xavier's teammates comes over.

"Clara," Ashton says and hugs me. "I heard you're on a layover. Lucky you get to join our fun-filled night." He laughs because they're obviously not doing much. "This is my girl, Kara."

I shake hands with the cute brunette. "Nice to meet you," she says.

Kara and I sit at the high-top table, and the boys start the dart game.

"You're a breath of fresh air after…" She looks over her shoulder. "Xavier's girlfriend, the model. We were so different, but you seem normal."

I try to pull my dress down as far as I can, but the thing doesn't budge. I am not as comfortable as Chevelle is in her skin. "I'm just a librarian from a small town. Nothing special."

"Are you kidding me? You know how many hot dreams I've had about librarians? Do you wear glasses at work?" Ben asks, reaching across me to get his drink. His cologne smells crisp and woodsy, and although I wasn't immediately attracted to him, I kind of feel like maybe I could get there.

"When I go to bed," I answer and laugh.

Kara rolls her eyes at Ben. "You're a Neanderthal," she says, clearly joking.

"What do you do?" I ask Kara.

She waves dismissively.

"Oh, make her tell you," Ashton says.

"I'm not embarrassed by it, it's just you jocks think it's so awesome." Kara smiles and looks at me. "I work for a sex toy company."

"Oh, that's awesome. Do you get free samples?" I ask, completely jealous.

"Yeah. My boss is the best. She says we can't sell them to the masses if we don't use them on our ourselves first."

"Share the wealth sometime."

"She can share them all because she's got me now and I'm bigger than all those vibrators she gets," Ashton says.

"You know it, babe." Kara gives me an expression as if to say, *Whatever, I just go with it.* Then she leans in and says under her breath, "Men are such simple creatures."

We both laugh, and it's nice. There were times when I'd come down to see Xavier play and I didn't feel as though I fit in because I was just the friend and not the girlfriend. It's amazing how bitchy and snotty players' wives can be.

After the boys take their turn, they hand over the darts and Kara and I step up to the line. I score our team sixty points with a twenty triple with one throw.

"Whoa!" Ben says. "Look at my girl."

I'm not his girl, but maybe a small part of me wants revenge after my last time here in San Francisco. To show Xavier he can't dictate my life for me, especially if I don't say boo about his.

"You're a hustler," Ashton says.

"I never told you I couldn't play, you assumed." I bat my eyes innocently.

Kara high-fives me.

"We should've known, dude. She's X's friend and none of us have ever beaten him," Ben says.

"Truth. Probably 'cause that's all there is to do up in Alaska, huh?" Ashton asks with good humor.

"You're from Alaska?" Kara looks excited now. "I've always wanted to go. It looks so beautiful."

Another difference, because when the other girlfriends and wives found out I was from Alaska, they acted as though I must live off the land.

"What's going on over here?" Xavier comes by with his siblings and the grandmas.

"We have next game," Midge says and puts a quarter on the table.

Everyone looks at it for a moment, not understanding.

"It holds our place," she says as if we're all idiots.

"Okay," I say. "We're almost done. I'm about to declare this game over."

"God, I love that my girl has such confidence." Ben rubs his palms together and grins.

"Your girl?" Xavier asks with an arched eyebrow.

My back is to Xavier, so I concentrate on the dartboard, desperately wanting to finish this game. I like the attention Ben gives me, but I also know how much of a wedge it could put between him and Xavier and they're just starting their season.

"Yeah. You know I've had a thing for Clara for a while now."

"You have?" Chevelle asks.

"Who wouldn't?"

I throw my three darts in rapid succession to get it over with and turn around to see Mandi's eyes on Xavier. I shake my head.

"We won," I say since no one is paying attention to the game.

Ben jumps up and picks me up, swinging me around. "What can't you do?"

Seriously, I need to keep him around me for the ego boost alone.

Once he lowers my feet to the floor, I mumble, "I'm going to the bathroom."

Thankfully, neither Mandi nor Chevelle follow, because I just want to be by myself. But that doesn't last, because while I'm washing my hands, the door of the bathroom opens, and Xavier stands there.

"What?" I turn off the tap.

"Do you like him? Honestly. No bullshit. No doing it out of spite. Do you like him?" His gaze is hard, and I realize how much I miss the affable guy I used to spend so much time with.

I rip off the paper towel to dry my hands. "I barely know him. And frankly, Xavier, I'm not sure it's any of your business."

He blows out a breath. "It's not. I know that. But I want to know. Because he has a reputation."

I laugh. "Yours isn't much better."

He nods. "Fair enough. But I don't want you to get hurt."

My eyes narrow on him. "You mean again. You hurt me, so you don't want someone else to do it too because that would somehow make you feel more guilty for hurting me? Well…" I toss the paper towel in the trash. "You're off the hook. I'm not sad anymore, Xavier. Sure, I miss our friendship, but that's all." I go to walk by him, but he blocks the door.

"Clara, I'm sorry."

"Seriously, take your sorry and shove it up your ass." I push by him and walk out of the bathroom—right into a broad chest.

Ben.

Seriously?

"Hey, is X in there?" He points toward the women's room.

"Yep, have at it."

He actually walks into the women's restroom, and I wonder what constitutes crossing the line for these football players.

Not even a minute goes by before Ben is at my side as I head to the bar. "Hey, I just asked X and he's cool with it, so I wanted to know if I could maybe get your number?"

I stop at an empty table. Xavier comes out of the bathroom, walking right by the both of us with his head down. I shouldn't feel a stab of guilt, but it's there nonetheless.

"Sure, give me your phone." I hold out my hand.

I give Ben my number, knowing he'll probably never use it. After all, Xavier said he was cool with it, right? And what Xavier says goes.

Chapter Twelve

Xavier

*W*atching Clara with Ben isn't a great feeling. Sure, I've seen Clara with guys before. Who wouldn't be interested in her? But now my own teammate is asking for her number, and if he breaks her heart, I'll have to break him. Which is a problem since he's got about fifty pounds and two inches on me. But Clara is way too important to me not to try to protect her.

Ben had the nerve to ask me for her number after finding me in the women's bathroom she'd just come out of. Fuck him. What if I was trying to make a go of it with her?

Thankfully, after the number exchange and flirting over the darts, my family is tired and wants to head back to their hotel. I say my goodbyes, having another awkward encounter with Clara when doing so, and head back to my condo alone.

By the time I'm home, I'm restless, unsure what to do to get rid of this feeling. It's why I love being in San Francisco more than Sunrise Bay these days. Because I don't have to think about her or what went wrong and why our friendship took a nosedive.

I fall into my couch and grab my remote, turning on the sports channel. There's Guilia, standing beside some Italian race car driver named Andrea. Just looking at them, I can see that they fit much better than she and I ever did.

My phone vibrates in my pocket, and I pull it out, seeing my dad's name.

"Hey, Dad," I answer. I always answer now.

"How's the season looking?"

I talk to him about the drills, how I feel slow and probably should've done more in the off-season. He assures me this is my year, but I'm just not feeling it. I don't tell him that though. My mind is in too many goddamn places.

"I heard you had some family down by you tonight?"

"Yeah. It was nice to see everyone."

"That's good. I guess the vacation was a success. Next time we both get to go on it."

"I'm there," I say, because I made a commitment to myself this past summer that I'd be there for my family. I'm not going to let myself be distracted from what's important in my life again. Guilia isn't at fault, but she definitely wasn't a fan of small-town Alaska. She likes the bright lights and exclusive clubs.

"Good."

Neither of us says anything for a moment.

"Dad?" Knowing him, he already knows what I'm about to ask.

"Yeah?"

"You know that saying 'let them go and if they come back, they're yours?'"

He chuckles. "It's something like that. What about it?"

"Do you think it's true?"

"Is this about who I think it's about?"

I'm not sure where my dad and Marla stand on the whole Clara thing. As far as I know, she's told no one what went down.

"Yeah." I nod even though he can't see me.

"Son, I remember when you were little, and her mother and I had to discuss sleepovers and whether we should stop them between you two. Now you're old enough to have sleepovers, but with all that comes the kind of decisions that adults face. I'm not sure what went down with you two, but I know she's been a great friend to you and you in return. But don't mistake missing her for something else. My advice is to be very careful with how you proceed and don't make a rash decision."

"But—"

"Xavier, you're the type of guy who goes for what he wants without thinking much of consequences. Always have been. You're hell-bent that you're always right, and as great of a quarterback as that makes you, you can't deal with people's feelings that way."

"Didn't you go after Marla?"

He chuckles. "It seems that way to you, but we were careful. We each had our own kids to consider. Yours and Clara's lives are weaved in with so many other people who you care about. Just make sure that whatever you want, you're positive you want it."

I sit for a moment and process what he's saying, pushing a hand through my hair. "Thanks, Dad."

"You're welcome. Now go out there and be the Super Bowl-winning quarterback I know you are."

I laugh. "I will."

We hang up after saying I love you, and I can't help but think my dad somehow just knew I needed him and his wisdom tonight.

I open up my contacts, and when I see the date on our last exchange, I can't believe it's been this long since I've texted Clara. How have I survived our drought?

I stare at the screen for a long time, then close it because my dad is right.

But I open it back up two minutes later. Fuck that, I know what I'm doing. I've trusted my gut my entire career, why wouldn't I now?

So I start simple.

> You looked good tonight.

Three dots appear, and I wait to see what she'll come back with.

The End

ALSO BY PIPER RAYNE

The Baileys

Lessons from a One-Night Stand (FREE)

Advice from a Jilted Bride

Birth of a Baby Daddy

Operation Bailey Wedding (Novella)

Falling for My Brother's Best Friend

Demise of a Self-Centered Playboy

Confessions of a Naughty Nanny

Operation Bailey Babies (Novella)

Secrets of the World's Worst Matchmaker

Winning my Best Friend's Girl

Rules for Dating Your Ex

Operation Bailey Birthday (Novella)

The Greene Family

My Twist of Fortune (Free Prequel)

My Beautiful Neighbor (FREE)

My Almost Ex

My Vegas Groom

A Greene Family Summer Bash (Novella)

My Sister's Flirty Friend

My Unexpected Surprise

My Famous Frenemy

A Greene Family Vacation (Novella)

My Scorned Best Friend

My Fake Fiancé

My Brother's Forbidden Friend

A Greene Family Christmas (Novella)

Lake Starlight

The Problem with Second Chances

The Issue with Bad Boy Roommates

The Trouble with Runaway Brides

The Drawback of Single Dads

Plain Daisy Ranch

One Last Summer

The One I Left Behind

The One I Stood Beside

The One I Didn't See Coming

Modern Love

Charmed by the Bartender

Hooked by the Boxer

Mad about the Banker

Single Dads Club

Real Deal

Dirty Talker

Sexy Beast

Hollywood Hearts

Mister Mom

Animal Attraction

Domestic Bliss

Bedroom Games

Cold as Ice

On Thin Ice

Break the Ice

Chicago Law

Smitten with the Best Man

Tempted by my Ex-Husband

Seduced by my Ex's Divorce Attorney

Blue Collar Brothers

Flirting with Fire

Crushing on the Cop

Engaged to the EMT

White Collar Brothers

Sexy Filthy Boss

Dirty Flirty Enemy

Wild Steamy Hook-up

The Rooftop Crew

My Bestie's Ex

A Royal Mistake

The Rival Roomies

Our Star-Crossed Kiss

The Do-Over

A Co-Workers Crush

Hockey Hotties

Countdown to a Kiss (Free Prequel)

My Lucky #13 (FREE)

The Trouble with #9

Faking it with #41

Tropical Hat Trick (Novella)

Sneaking around with #34

Second Shot with #76

Offside with #55

Kingsmen Football Stars

False Start (Free Prequel)

You Had Your Chance, Lee Burrows

You Can't Kiss the Nanny, Brady Banks

Over My Brother's Dead Body, Chase Andrews

Chicago Grizzlies

On the Defense (Free Prequel)

Something like Hate

Something like Lust

Something like Love

The Nest

Mr. Heartbreaker

Mr. Broody

Mr. S (Title to be revealed)

Mr. C (Title to be revealed)

Holiday Romances

Single and Ready to Jingle

Claus and Effect

Merry Kissmas

Cockamamie Unicorn Ramblings

We love doing these little novellas in between the full-length books. Originally, it was supposed to involve the entire Greene family, but without realizing it, timeline wise we had Presley giving birth to Leighton and Hank was sick. Then we had to figure out how to get Xavier involved since the football season had started. Layover for the win!

And originally, Dori and Midge were not going to go, but what kind of vacation would it be without our three favorite grandmas!

We hope you enjoyed reading as much as we enjoyed writing. This was really a fun project to work on and you know how much we LOVE to tease you! We wouldn't be Piper Rayne if we didn't! There's a lot to cover in the last three books of the series so get strapped in for the ride!

Big thanks to the following...
Everyone at the Valentine PR Team
Cassie from Joy Editing for line edits.
Ellie from My Brother's Editor for line edits.
Rosa from My Brother's Editor for proofreading.
Hang Le for the cover and branding for the entire series. Those colors!
Bloggers who consistently carve out time to read, review and/or promote our work.
Piper Rayne Unicorns who hang out with us in our Facebook group and love these little families we create as much as we do! Thank you!

Every reader who took the time to read our story. We're more grateful than we can ever say.

Who doesn't love Childhood friends to lover's trope? Xavier and Clara were best friends all their life until they weren't. If Xavier wants to make amends, he's got a lot of work and groveling to do. Good thing the Greene men aren't afraid to fight for the women they love. We can't wait to see how it will unfold!

xo,
Piper & Rayne

ABOUT PIPER & RAYNE

Piper Rayne is a USA Today Bestselling Author duo who write "heartwarming humor with a side of sizzle" about families, whether that be blood or found. They both have e-readers full of one-clickable books, they're married to husbands who drive them to drink, and they're both chauffeurs to their kids. Most of all, they love hot heroes and quirky heroines who make them laugh, and they hope you do, too!